WINNER AND THE POACHER

WINNER AND THE
POACHER

A PORTIA OAKESHOTT, DINOSAUR
VETERINARIAN SHORT NOVEL

RAYMUND EICH

1

The self-driving rideshare sedan turned off the coast road. On whispers of the electric motor and smooth living asphalt, the sedan carried its passenger between marble colonnades to the neighborhood's entry gate. The bar was down and the sedan obediently stopped and opened its window. Mild latewinter air drifted in, tanged with salt, and bearing the rustle of waves on rocks.

A speaker in the gate kiosk spoke in a firm male voice. "Your name, and who to see."

"Portia Oakeshott. The police called me to 17 Aldersley Lane." The gate bar failed to lift. "I'm with the dino company."

The bar lifted then. The sedan rolled forward, down dark and winding streets nearly empty though it was about 1300 of the local clock. On either side, bathed in the orange-red glow of sunlamps, rambling houses sprawled across vast lots, set back behind towering oaks and wide front lawns, grass cropped as low as a golf fairway's or a footy oval's. The houses invariably faced tall windows to the northern horizon, craving Stella Australis A, last seen two weeks before.

Thank God the sun would rise in just a couple of days.

But not today.

The sedan came to a T-junction, beyond which, and through a grove of eucalyptus in someone's side yard, a faint glimmer of twilight showed the seam between sky and ocean. A right turn, then a stop, three houses ahead. Long but not low. A shed roof sloped north, away from the street.

With a thought through her neuronal interface, Portia transferred two cryptoquid and climbed out. The crash of waves overwhelmed the sound of motor and street as the sedan drove off for its next passenger.

She studied the southern face of the house. Windowless. Doorless? No, follow the flagstones to that gap in the curtain wall, near the west side. The soles of her flats snapped on the pavers. Electric torches flanking the gap pivoted and flooded her with light.

She stopped squinting just as a uniformed policeman emerged from the gap. A round face, jug ears. He gave her an appraising glance up and down. "Sorry, miss. Police business. Please move along."

Portia stopped and crossed her arms. "I'm with the dino company."

The policeman started. He glanced to the side, the common gesture of someone looking up information. "You're Dr. Oakeshott? I was expecting, y'know, some old bloke with the brim snapped up on his digger hat."

"You have me."

The policeman swallowed. "Inspector Leichhardt is expecting you. He's in the lower basement. Go in, turn right, service corridor, fourth door on your right."

Portia went three steps past the policeman and in.

Double doors opened into a gigantic living room, extending the full depth of the house to picture windows facing the twilit ocean. An open sliding glass door let in the sounds of surf and muttering policemen standing on a balcony. The ceiling was vaulted to the sloped roof and striped with skylights. The furniture, all straight lines with a color palette mixing grayscale and natural wood, had the 99% perfect look of bespoke handcrafting.

A rich man's house, if the drive in hadn't tipped her.

She followed the policeman's instructions to the stairwell down. A din of echoes off walls excavated from rock and concrete stairs. At the first landing, she glimpsed a rec room. Picture windows blended with the rock face of the bluff. Billiards, air hockey, robotic craps and blackjack tables. Half-empty liquor glasses and spent vape canisters barnacled each tabletop, like Mesozoic fungi and mosses growing in the dinosaur preserve a thousand klicks to the south.

A rich man's party, interrupted. That might explain the police.

But why a dinosaur veterinarian?

The stairwell ended another five meters down. Bulbs flashed on the other side of a half-open door. Portia sniffed but smelled neither alcohol nor blood. She approached with hesitant steps, and rapped her knuckles on the door.

"Dr. Oakeshott?" A man's voice, smooth and slow. "Come in."

She went into the room. For a moment, her heart seemed to stop.

A space as large as the living room or the rec room, but windowless. And stuffed with mounted dinosaurs. In the middle, dioramas of small and bird-like creatures. A geiersaur's hooked beak ripping flesh from the belly of a minmi flipped on its back like a giant turtle A grackelsaur snapping a millipede into the air and just touching its jaws to it, prior to swallowing it whole.

Along the walls, mounted heads. There, another minmi, its stolid face surrounded with bony protrusions like an elizabeth collar. There, a strallo, a male *Australovenator*, the bumps on his nasal ridge as bright red-orange as a spring sunset after a volcanic eruption.

Mounted dinosaurs. About two dozen of them.

Yes, the company granted hunting permits, both to thin the numbers of species pushing the preserve's carrying capacity and to bring in revenue from tourists, especially off-worlders. And the taxidermists had respected the trophies enough to pose them true to life, and not dress them in schoolboy uniforms to play cricket. Still, these creatures deserved better. Especially—

Her breath caught. On the far wall, a head so huge it seemed impossible to belong to a once-living creature—

"I don't know those huge plant-eaters well enough," said the man. "Is that a winner or a tina?"

Wintonotitan can be distinguished from the preserve's other titanosaur, Diamantinasaurus, by its broader face and more gracile bone structure.

Wintonotitan's skin is a darker green and may have brownish patches, most commonly on the legs and....

Rehearsing the field guidebook lifted her above flooding emotions for a moment, until she gave the mounted head a closer look. The soft jaw. A mottled spot like a fallen leaf on the sloping brow above the eyes. Her stomach clenched. "A winner cow."

A light strobed somewhere. Portia squeezed shut her eyes.

"Y'know," the man said, "we should let the forensic techs finish taking photos and so on while we talk more."

She opened her eyes enough to see him gesture at the door.

"After you, Dr. Oakeshott." He plainly sensed her unease but didn't want to call her out on it.

She kept her eyes on the half-open door. Easy to do when your vision is turning gray and spotty in the periphery. The crack of her flat soles on concrete treads brought her back enough that she reached ground level without incident, and entered the first room she found.

Motion-activated lights revealed a kitchen, gleaming with stainless steel and gray-black granite. She pulled out a stool and sat at an island counter, where small but heavy-looking appliances sat next to a black glass induction cooktop covered with used glasses and empty beer bottles.

The man followed her. A sticky sound meant he'd trod through spilled beer. He leaned his elbows on the island and angled his head at a paddle full of holes mounted on extra-large stand mixer. "My missus might know what that's for, but I haven't a clue."

She inhaled deeply, and though the stale odors of last night's party filled her nose, the air was fresh enough for her to fully recover. "I'm sorry, I've assumed you're Inspector Leichhardt, but I didn't ask to be certain."

"Quite all right, Doctor. We threw you in the deep end down there."

"I'm pronouncing it correctly? 'Like-heart.'"

"Bang on. Alan Leichhardt, Port Bounty Police." Brown hair salted with gray, brown eyes radiating fine wrinkles from their outer corners. He pushed off the counter and extended his hand. A crisp white cuff extended out of the sleeve of a mass-market blue suit. She shook a hand patterned with calluses.

Her glance darted around the room. "What happened?"

"You can tell, they were having a blowout, everyone's got a gutful, when we got called about a...." He licked his lips and his eyes studied the grain of the granite while he answered. "Can't go into details, ongoing investigation, y'know."

Her cheeks warmed. Something lurid. "And?"

"We're investigating. Then a straggler with boots so wobbly he didn't run off when police were coming pipes up. 'Don't let them see the second basement.' That's probable cause right there. We go down. Pick the lock. And realize we need an expert."

The company granted hunting rights on the preserve, but only when a species needed its numbers managed. Never had the company allowed hunting of winner cows. That stuffed head in the lower basement... Portia shivered. Then through the balcony door and the mansion's open floor plan came the muttered words of the other policemen and the crash of waves on rocks at the base of the bluff. "Was dinosaur poaching the worst crime committed here last night?"

He leaned his elbows on the counter and regarded her with his wrinkled brown eyes. "As you guessed, it wasn't. See, we've locked horns with this fella for years, on stuff that's not quite as—" Leichhardt's tongue darted between his lips and he glanced down. "Every time his father bails him out and lawyers him up. You from Port Bounty, miss—doctor?"

She shook her head. "Esperance Heights, on Cookland." Trees lined with oaks and sweetgums, and the sun rose every day, even in the weeks of winter.

"You wouldn't know the pull the Martinson family has around here, then," Leichhardt said. "The pattern repeated last night. Young Lachlan Martinson went american on us—"

"American?"

"Y'know, like the costume dramas set centuries ago on Earth." Leichhardt put on a funny accent. "'I decline to answer and I'd like to speak with my attorney.' And he won't turn over audio or video from his neuronal interface, and we can't compel him to." He wrinkled his nose, as if the odor of spilled beer had gotten to him. "Importing all that American nonsense into proper Anglo-Australian criminal procedure. There's a reason the Americans lost their hyper-power status...."

He took a breath and his expression softened. "Brambles in the path, mate," he muttered to himself. "Where was I, Dr. Oakeshott?"

"You've never convicted Lachlan Martinson of any other crime he's committed."

"Bang on. And what happened last night." Leichhardt nodded in the direction of the balcony. "We can't let Martinson, or whichever of his guests did it, walk free. So we realized the dinosaurs might be a way to ring him up, like Capone on tax."

Her brow wrinkled.

"Figure of speech. Get him on something minor. Then we use that as a wedge to ring him up on everything else."

"Dinosaur poaching being the wedge." As if that dead winner cow counted for nothing.

He's not saying that. She counts for something, but less than whatever a person suffered here last night.

"Not to make light of it," Leichhardt said, "but bang on. We know under Dinosaur Hunting Act 2749 that your company only allows hunting on the preserve under permit specifying species and sex, and logs DNA information on animals taken. Should be dead simple to see which ones Martinson's taken without permit."

She knew the gist of the Act, but called up the text through her neuronal interface and skimmed it where it was projected on the finger-print-smudged stainless steel refrigerator door. "He's got an obvious defense. Claim they wandered off the preserve. It's open season then."

"The preserve's got fencing, right?"

Portia shook her head. "It's got a double line of perimeter markers a hundred meters apart. They have passive measures, shape and color striping, that the dinosaurs have been genetically coded to avoid. They react to motion of dinosaurs off the preserve with sirens, ultrasonics, flashing lights, and stench bombs. And shoot video. And the farmers adjoining the preserve invariably run fencing along the back lines of their properties."

Leichhardt rubbed his fingertips against the base of their thumb. "From all that...."

"Martinson could claim the dinosaurs wandered off the preserve, but he'd be lying. Our records would prove it."

His voice sounded smoother than usual. "I'm with you, that the dinos didn't just up and go walkabout."

Portia's next words hurried out. "And I know that's a winner cow, and we've never granted a hunting permit for one. You have all you need to, how did you put it? Ring him up?"

The police inspector showed a callused palm. "We're on the right track, but we need more. Yes, doctor, you can tell a winner from a tina, but twelve random subjects of His Majesty? They'll want DNA evidence."

"Simple enough to provide," Portia said, but then a chill gripped her. How much DNA had survived taxidermy?

The cold sensation faded. She could research the matter online, or she could turn to the crime scene team. Police forensics techs must have more experience with extracting DNA from real-world samples than anyone.

"Our people would love to," Leichhardt said, "but they can't amplify dino DNA. Something about not having the, what are those doovalackies called? PCR primers for it. So we'll have to deputize the sequencing to your company."

"That shouldn't be a problem," Portia said, then wondered what she might've just committed the company to do.

His brown eyes fixed on her face. "Blockchain of custody is crucial. Martinson's lawyer will look for any moment when the samples left your sight between here and your DNA sequencing apparatus, in a bid to gin up reasonable doubt in a jury's mind. And your sequencing apparatus better have a proper maintenance history from the moment it rolled out of the fabricator."

"I understand."

"You're going to have to agree to share the inputs from your eyes and ears to your optic and auditory nerves through your neuronal interface into the planetary law enforcement blockchain. From the moment we hand you skin samples from the mounted dinos to the moment they enter your DNA sequencer. Do you agree?"

"I'll still be able to communicate privately through my neury?"

"If you don't speak out loud, yeah."

And with the information the company would provide the police, Martinson would face a penalty. The winner cow, and all the others, slain and skinned to make the cabinet of grotesqueries two levels below, would receive some justice. "Let's begin."

"Here's how you access the law enforcement blockchain." Leichhardt slipped his badge holder from his suit jacket's breast pocket. He flipped the badge up to reveal a QR code. "Run that through your neury."

She stared at the QR code until words formed in her vision. Black text crossed her view of flat-front cupboards. *Royal New New South Wales Law Enforcement Consortium Electronic Evidence Blockchain. You are hereby granted write-only access by Insp. Alan Leichhardt, Port Bounty PD, for the upload of personal audio and video recordings, relating to....*

Portia read the rest, then nodded. Her neury popped a winking red *REC* icon in the lower left corner of her vision, next to icons of a video camera and a microphone.

Leichhardt stood straight. "For the record, your name?"

"Portia Oakeshott. DVM."

"Your employer?"

"Blighland Dinosaur Preserve." Should she add the legal jargon at the back? "Proprietary Limited."

"Thank you, Dr. Oakeshott. I shall now take you to a location where we found evidence of a violation of Dinosaur Hunting Act 2749...."

Back to the lower basement. Amid the mounted bodies and body parts, Portia remained steadier on her feet. When she regarded the dead dinosaurs, the flipped minmi, the brightly-colored strallo, all the others, the winner cow's head most of all, dread and disgust were now alloyed with anger. The company's work—combining fossil evidence, bird DNA, educated guesswork, and Aussie pride—being exploited to serve some man's vanity—

The resident of this house had worked a vile crime, and she would do her part to make him pay.

Leichhardt introduced her to a forensics tech, a woman with tiny jowls and brown hair wisping out of a bun. "I'll cut and bag the samples," she said. Her voice was kindly and gritted by four or five decades of use. "How much do you need?"

"A picogram should be sufficient."

Wrinkles deepened around her eyes. "Field versus lab, and how much gets lost in tanning," she muttered to herself. "Got it."

The tech went from dinosaur to dinosaur, Portia in tow. With a whining rotary cutter, the tech cut one-centimeter squares of leatherized skin from the underside of each mounted figure. Each square went in a plastic baggie with an embedded RFID chip as the tech asked, "And this one is?"

Portia rattled off both the scientific and the common names, and each dinosaur's sex, if she could tell. The winner cow wasn't the only one that could not have been taken lawfully.

The tech nodded at each of Portia's identifications. When she had a sample, she sealed the square in its baggie and stared at the RFID chip. Portia's neury picked up the encoding of each chip by sounding a ding in her mind's ear and popping into her vision a call-out box with the dinosaur's identification and a timestamp. The tech clicked the rotary cutter's head into a handheld UV sterilizer as they went to the next mounted dinosaur.

"You've been in this line of work a while?" Portia asked over the hum of the sterilizer.

"Come back part-time after my youngest started primary school. Righty, now who's this bonzer bloke?"

They looked up at the winner cow. "That's a female winner. *Wintonotitan novacambrianovaaustraliensis*." Portia's knees suddenly felt weak. She leaned her hand on the wall and sucked in a breath.

"Stay with me, doctor."

Portia drew in another breath, then nodded and stood tall again. "I remember, when I was a girl of five or six standard, we visited a couple who were friends of my parents. He hunted, not dinos, but the usual creatures stocked on Cookland. Emus, kangaroos. I wandered into his den and found a full roo mounted like—" She waved slender fingers at the minmi and the geiersaur.

"At first I thought it was a toy. Then I saw a bullethole in the chest and I thought the roo, he'd embalmed it, skin, flesh, bone, all, like the mummies on Pharaon." She shivered. "I had nightmares for weeks."

"It's just skin," the tech said.

"My father explained that to me...." Portia's legs wobbled again. Somewhere, a thousand kilometers to the south, lay a dead winner cow with its head skinned. Or had they skinned the entire carcass? She hadn't seen the resident's closet, how many leather jackets and pairs of cowboy boots had been made from the winner cow? Or, like they once did with elephants, had they turned her feet into meter-wide footstools?

The tech ducked under the placid head. She extended the rotary cutter to the underside of the winner's neck, where it met the wall. A brief whine, a zip as plastic sealed. The sounds grounded Portia back in the room. They moved on.

Though her legs felt steady, Portia avoided looking at the winner cow head as they finished their work.

After twenty minutes, they finished. The tech handed her a duffel bag marked *Property of PBPD*. All the samples inside barely weighted down the bag. Still, she trudged up the echoing concrete stairs. A young man so rich he could throw a monster party on a Twoday night, so scornful of the laws under which his family had prospered. It wasn't right. Not one bit.

She mulled these thoughts as another rideshare sedan took her, and the duffel bag on the seat next to her, out of the neighborhood. In places where the coast highway ran with only a guardrail between it and crashing waves, twilight glimmered to her left, a hair brighter than before. Maybe the weeks of winter made bad actors think darkness covered their crimes.

Actors. Plural. The spoiled rich resident of that house wouldn't have the skill or patience for taxidermy, too right.

After two kilometers eastward on the coast highway, toward the lighted highrises of downtown Port Bounty, the sedan turned right. Another two klicks brought her to the front gate of the company's campus. The gate recognized her and rose, allowing the rideshare in without stopping.

The sedan followed an asphalt lane flowing past sweetgums and oaks and along the terrain's contours to the main building. Blocks of quarried native stone gave the building an ancient dignity, like the public buildings seen in the background of a costume drama set in ancient Australia during the First World War. But the cameras and sensors tracking her entrance and the whisper of the doors sliding open for her approach were quite modern.

Portia carried the duffel bag over her shoulder to the wing of veterinary offices and labs. The sequencing lab hummed with machinery and air con. She shut the door behind her, then found the newest sequencer and checked its maintenance logs through her neury. As clean as the machine's molded plastic housing.

Satisfied, she got to work. The sequencer could handle eight samples at a time. Through her neury, she told the sequencer each sample's species and that it was tanned hide. Then she pressed *start*.

Lights flashed on the control panel and status messages crossed the screen. *Extracting DNA from leather... Determining species-specific primers... Amplification cycle 1....*

Ninety seconds later, the screen flicked to *Amplification cycle 2....*

Forty cycles of exponential duplication to get enough DNA for sequencing. Sequencing itself would be quick, but it would still take three sequencer runs to process all the samples.

Four hours later, the machine sounded a little fanfare. Final run complete. Data transferred to redundant and tamper-proof storage. Copied to the planet-wide police blockchain.

A message from Leichhardt de-deputized her. Gladly she stopped recording what she saw and heard. No journo she.

Freed, Portia requested a copy of the third run of sequences. She had a hunch from the first two runs, and wanted to see—

Knuckles rapped on the door.

"Come in," she called, expecting another veterinarian or a field ecologist.

The door opened. Portia's eyebrows jumped. Not a tech. Black hair low down his forehead, tailored gray suit accented with a bright yellow pocket square, body like a boxer from a light weight class. Pietrangelo, the company's chief operations officer.

Quickly she stood. "Mr. Pietrangelo, what brings you here?"

"I wanted to get a report from you. Had lunch? We'll hit the esky for some tucker."

"Sir, I..." She'd sat in the back of meetings he'd led, but in her three local years, six months standard, with the company, she'd never interacted with him face to face.

"On my quid. Come along." Not a command, exactly, but she followed without hesitation.

Pietrangelo strode down the corridors like a ship boosting at one *gee* for space far enough from stars and planets to enter hyperdrive. A powerful man. Portia pulled her arms closer. Her mother had warned her, powerful men could make a young lady devalue her virtue. But Pietrangelo's power flowed down proper channels, making the company run better, and protecting the dinosaurs on the preserve.

Didn't it?

The lunch room featured mass-produced plastic chairs and tables. One person, Alex the lead coder, ate alone. Veterinary director Hawkins and the other female vet, blond and sun-freckled Tiana Spence, broke off their conversation at the sight of Pietrangelo and hustled empty trays to the recycling hopper on their way out the door.

The esky, a cluster of storing, cooking, and serving modules, took up most of the back wall. No one waited at any of the order kiosks or tray dispensers. She went to the Mediterranean station, normally the most popular. Where was everyone? Her stomach growled and she double-checked the time. Nineteen o'clock, two hours after the main lunch hour at noon of New New South Wales' thirty-four hour day.

She sat near the window with a Greek salad, chicken shawarma, and hot tea steeping in a cup. Pietrangelo joined her, carrying a tray of spiced, orange-red meat grounds on lettuce boats and a mug of thick black coffee. Before he took his first bite, he asked, "Tell me what you've found so far."

"I've finished sequencing all twenty-three samples taken from the suspect's collection."

Muscles flexed at Pietrangelo's jaw hinges. He shook his head and spoke around a mouthful. "I saw that already. Have you looked at the data?"

"Yes. Who wouldn't?"

A swallow, then, "Notice anything?"

"Ten samples are from species we've never permitted for hunting. The winner, the—you've got the list?"

"Yeah. And I've checked records from the field offices. None of those species have crossed the perimeter since the suspect grew hair on his, ah, body."

"He took them on the preserve." Warmth filled her torso. "That's all the proof the police need."

Pietrangelo angled his head. "Probably, but tell me more."

"The snips showing where we released their founding generations are almost all from the sector near the town of Blenheim."

Pietrangelo regarded her in silence for a moment. Her mouth turned dry. Had she made a mistake?

Snips—single nucleotide polymorphisms—existed in nature because of the genetic code's redundancy. Some random mutations left intact the function of an encoded protein. In human and natural animal populations, snips served as markers of ethnicity and—her cheeks warmed—paternity.

When the company raised a stock of eggs and hatchlings for release, the genetic engineers created sets of snips encoding data relating to that stock. Among that encoded data, time and place of release into the preserve. She'd double-checked the data extracted by the sequencer against the company's records. Near the town of Blenheim. No doubt.

"*Almost* all?"

"The only exception was a geiersaur, released in the next sector, south of Margarettown."

"And the only flier." Pietrangelo reached for his coffee. "One might call that a clue."

Tension bled from Portia's shoulders. "The suspect hunted in the sector near Blenheim," she said, voice bright. "And that's where the police should look for the taxidermist."

"Good thought." Pietrangelo lifted a lettuce boat of spiced meat. Coriander, cumin? Portia's nose couldn't tell. "You can talk about it with them."

Puzzlement wrinkled the skin between her eyes. "I've told Inspector Leichhardt all I know."

"I'm certain of that, but Blenheim is a thousand klicks out of his jurisdiction. We've called in the Royal Frontier Police."

Portia's eyes went wide. "The frontos?"

"Think that's what I said. And in fact—" Pietrangelo turned his head. She read the gesture as him checking something through his neury. "Oh bugger, he's early." He crammed another lettuce boat into his mouth in two bites, then grabbed his mug of black coffee by the handle. "Come along, doctor. You can bring your tea."

Portia carried her half-full tray to the recycler with one hand, her cuppa with the other. Pietrangelo stalked through the halls to the elevators. She hurried to keep up.

His office filled a corner of the top floor. Dimly visible through reflections in the windows were the racked lights of skycrapers downtown on one side and the campus' hatcheries and utility buildings on the other.

A man with broad shoulders waited in a leather-upholstered chair in front of Pietrangelo's wide, true-wood desk. The stranger wore brown hair close to his scalp, and Portia couldn't decide if he had enough stubble on his jaw and chin to call it a beard. He had bags under his eyes. From the outdated cut and color palette, his slacks, shirt, and vest could have come from the same tailor as her father.

He stood up. The badge flipped open at his vest pocket flashed a reflection at her eyes. "G'day. Special Agent Lamar Dowling, RFP." The flow of his voice made her revise his age downward. Thirty standard. "Hope you don't mind, the expert system, artificial personality, whatever you call your virtual assistant let me in to wait."

"No worries," Pietrangelo said, and introduced himself. They shook hands like they were trying to crush each other's bones. Men.

With a wince, Pietrangelo broke off the handshake. "And this is Dr. Portia Oakeshott."

Dowling blinked heavily as he reached for her hand. He gripped it softly, with skin smoother than she expected. "Ph.D.?"

"DVM."

"Ripper. Wouldn't want to go on this trip with someone whose nose is up near the top of her ivory tower."

Portia bristled. Then frowned. "Trip?"

Dowling raised an eyebrow at Pietrangelo. "What have you told her?"

"Not much. She figured it out on her own." He went around his desk, to a chair with keypad-laden arms like those Portia imagined graced the bridge of a hyperdrive ship. "Everyone, have a seat."

She took one of the leather chairs facing the desk, Dowling the other. Though her skirt was hemmed at mid-calf, she kept her knees together and pointed away from the Frontier Police agent and twisted her upper body to face him. "You're going after the taxidermist."

Dowling turned his baggy eyes to her gaze. "And others, too. Our laired-up bastard took all the dinos from the same part of the preserve, right? Makes me think he's got helpers in or around Blenheim. Any guesses what kind of help they're giving him?"

"A tracker, perhaps? And a pilot. Someone with that much money wouldn't take ten or twelve hours to drive across Blighland when a charter aircraft could make the run in two. Wait, the pilot would be based here."

"Good thoughts." He peered at her, expecting more.

But what? Muscles bunched around her mouth... and then she remembered she wasn't at uni any more. These men weren't professors grading her. "A policeman can think of more than I can, I'm sure."

Special Agent Dowling bowed his head at the compliment. "Here's a big one that hadn't occurred to you. Where's the rest of the winner?"

The bridge of her nose wrinkled. "Somewhere in the preserve... where a field team might stumble on it? He dragged it off the preserve? No, the cameras didn't see it."

"My guess would be he buried it," said Dowling, "and that would take the devil's own long time with a shovel. He probably used a bulldozer."

"One can't sneak a bulldozer past the perimeter cameras," Portia said. Then her gaze darted to Pietrangelo. "Can one?"

Pietrangelo ran fingers between his neck and his shirt collar. "No, but we have bulldozers on the preserve, in the utility sheds at Hocknull Lodge."

"He broke into our facility?" Portia couldn't believe it. The way

Pietrangelo scowled at his coffee mug, and a world-weary expression flickered over Dowling's face, showed they didn't believe it either.

Her blood ran cold. With wobbly hands, she set her cuppa down on the desk before she spilled it. "A company employee helped him?"

"It's a possiblity we have to consider," Pietrangelo said. "If we've got a bad apple, I want to make a corker of an example of him to the other employees."

"And I'm looking for every angle I can to make a run at our suspect," added Dowling.

His words barely registered. She blinked around heat building around her eyes. "Of course," she said, more mildly than she felt. An employee flouting the company's mission.... She sniffed in a breath. Change your train of thought. "Special Agent, I see the need for you to investigate at Blenheim and Hocknull Lodge, but why do you want me on your trip?"

"I need a dino expert. We might have remains to identify, DNA to sequence, that sort of thing."

"I'm flattered," she said. She turned to Pietrangelo. "But many people here have more experience than I do. I've never been to Blenheim or Hocknull...." Her eyes widened.

Satisfaction sparked in Pietrangelo's dark eyes. "You're a sharp one, Dr. Oakeshott."

Dowling scratched the stubble on his jaw. "We'll go undercover. Perhaps as a tourist couple. I'll work up a story. Maybe newlyweds—"

Portia clamped her knees more tightly together and pointed them further away from the Frontier Police agent.

"—relax, doctor. Whenever I marry, it won't be to a wowser."

Her back stiffened. "I'm not a wowser." She knew how to have fun without a gutful of alcohol or a casual root.

Dowling rolled his eyes. "Can we book a two-room suite at the lodge?" he asked Pietrangelo.

"The suites are almost always booked far in advance. I can't pull the rug out from under a paying customer. You can try to reserve a suite right now, though it's buckley's chance one's available."

"I don't know when we'll get to the lodge," Dowling said. "We might not even visit the lodge at all. If we do, if a standard room has a couch long enough, that'll do me. Will that suffice, doctor?" Sarcasm spiced his last words.

She arched an eyebrow at him. "Barely."

Special Agent Dowling barked out a laugh. "You're a dinkum sheila, doctor."

Portia kept her eyebrow raised until Pietrangelo's pensive expression came through to her. "Sir?"

"We don't open the preserve to tourists till the day before vernal equinox," he said in his firm voice to Dowling. "2nd of Spring this year."

"Eight days from now." Dowling scratched his stubbly brown beard. "Word of the suspect's arrest will get out by then. His associates will cover their tracks, maybe even blow town. Any way to get down there now?"

"We do construction and maintenance work during the off-season. We can book you as contractors."

"It's got to be something that gives us an excuse to stay in Blenheim, if that's where the clues go."

"Too right," said Pietrangelo. "If I heard a contractor is blodging around off the preserve, I'd sack them immediately."

A hush descended. Portia picked up her cuppa from the desk. When she raised it to her lips, a thought worked loose. "Tourism consultants. The company hired us to review all aspects of the visitor experience, from the moment tourists step off the plane till they check out from the lodge."

Dowling's eyebrows quirked. "Clever. You sure you want to do this dino thing, Dr. Oakeshott? You might have a knack for police work."

Portia blinked. Images of mounted dinosaurs flashed on the inside of her eyelids. A tremble ran through her arms but thank God her tea stayed in its cup.

She swallowed around a tiny lump in her throat. "Veterinary work is the only job for me."

2
———

The panels overhead tried to give the aircraft's passengers the full spectrum of summer sunlight, but a glance out the windows dispelled the feeling. They flew through darkness, away from a dim smear of twiight, above a hidden landscape where the solitary lights of isolated farmsteads shone like lighthouses.

A spike of air pressure in Portia's ear informed her of their descent to Blenheim. The flap motors whined in the wings. The lights of the town filled the windows on the right. A small place, perhaps five thousand souls, but after overflying a thousand klicks of empty land, Blenheim seemed to stretch on like the glow of Endeavour Bay and New Canberra all rolled into one.

Tires chirped on asphalt. The landing jostled her against her shoulder belt. The engines hummed to slow them down, giving her a usual instant of worry that they'd overshoot the end of the runway. But the plane slowed and turned smoothly onto the taxiway, to the sighs and yawns of the half-dozen other passengers in the mostly empty cabin.

Dowling sat taller, which straightened some of the wrinkles in his size-too-big jacket. Zippers and carabiners clanked and clinked. He rubbed his baggy eyes. Around a yawn, he said, "I miss anything?"

"Bog standard descent," she said. "You slept solidly."

"Habit I learned in the Defense Force. Sleep when you can."

Her eyes widened. "You've been off-planet?"

"Days in one metal can followed by weeks in a larger one. The devil's own lack of glamour, let me tell you."

"But, you traveled in space...."

He laughed lightly. "I was military police stationed at Black Stump." A can-world, orbiting a gas giant, Watson, a billion kilometers away. Black Stump served as the main transshipment point for hyperdrive ships entering and leaving the Stella Australis system. "Spent most of my time tossing drunks into the back of the divvy van."

The aircraft rolled to the terminal. She glanced out the window and worry needled her. No other planes waited.... because she'd just arrived at a small town about a week before the tourist season. This wasn't Endeavour Bay's airport, with scores of departures and arrivals every day. She was lucky Blenheim had paved the runway.

Down a concourse lined with a tea kiosk, a fish-and-chips esky, the flashing lights of a gambling room, and a gift shop festooned with inaccurately-depicted stuffed dinosaurs. Behind the counters, bored girls chewed gum. Eyes ringed with too much makeup had the vacant looks of people engrossed by their neuries. Near the terminal exits, a skycap and his team of wheeled robots offered to carry their luggage to their car.

"Follow me," Dowling said. They went out the sliding doors.

Damp, chill air struck Portia's face. She hunched her shoulders and pulled in her neck. Thin fog diffused globular streetlights, shining at full power an hour before noon.

The special agent must have arranged their ride through his neury: a dark gray ute on raised tires rolled to the curb. It popped its doors. She climbed in while Dowling chatted with the skycap. Smells of leather and new car. She sat in one of the bucket seats in the rear. The robots slid their luggage into the ute's bed, next to the extended range battery under a rigid plastic tonneau cover. The skycap and his machines then returned to the warmth and light of the terminal.

Dowling joined her in the cabin, taking one of the rear-facing seats across from her. Ten centimeters separated their knees. Accent lights on the underside of the seats gave the cabin a cozy feeling. Portia pressed her knees together and angled them to the side. The ute shut its doors and rolled away from the terminal.

To say something, she asked, "Is this ute fronto standard issue?"

His seat back still adjusted to fit his broad shoulders. "No, I rented it as part of our cover."

"I hope I have it straight. We're pretending we're secret shoppers hired by the local tourism board, who are pretending they're a rich couple from Cookland?"

"Ripper."

"Can we practice more at the hotel?"

"We don't have time. It's already been thirty hours since I've gotten on the case. The taxidermist who mounted the winner cow and the other dinos might already have poured bleach and shone ultraviolet light on every square centimeter of his work area. If we wait till check-in time at the hotel, then practice, the local taxidermists will've closed up shop for the day, and we won't have a chance to question them till tomorrow morning. We've got to go now."

Portia fell silent. The ute traveled a two-lane road between a tobacco farm under growlights and a paddock of riddlepigs. "I'm not good at lying."

"You'll do fine, doctor."

Three taxidermists plied their trade in Blenheim. All looked the same from the outside: low buildings dressed in local stone, metal roofs, parking lots of gravel looking gray under security lights. Likewise inside. Sun-spectrum ceiling panels shown on lobbies with extruded plastic furniture, video frames looping outdoors scenes from the weeks of summer, and the stuffed full-sized skins of roos, pet dogs, and grackelsaurs.

Dowling played a hunter, come down from Cookland to meet and hire a guide for four days in Latesummer. With subtle shifts of voice, face, and posture, he looked and sounded ten years older and many fold richer. The grizzled men behind the counters, wearing thick aprons stained by chemicals, and not enough cologne to mask the odor of tanning agents, gave Portia appraising looks from the hem to the neck of her fitted dress, from mid-calf to collarbones.

The first time, after a moment of shock, she defiantly stood taller and canted her hip closer to Dowling. In the next two interviews, she put on the pose coming right out the gate. In all cases, the men glanced away from her and focused on Dowling with added respect.

Ten minutes with the first man, then the special agent thanked him and led Portia out. After the ute closed its doors and gravel crunched under the tires, she asked, "How can you tell it wasn't him?"

Dowling scratched his brown stubble. "I haven't been to church on a regular basis for many years, but there's a line that applies to my line of work. 'The guilty fleeth when no man pursueth.'"

Now that she had an inkling what to look for, the second man struck her as innocent from the start. A talkative old-timer, rambling about hunters he'd seen, reminscing about the earliest days of the preserve; but an expert at how best to process the hides of the different dinosaur species commonly brought to him by hunters.

"What about a winner?" Dowling asked casually.

"Ha'n't a clue. The company have never let any hunter take one."

Dowling shrugged his broad shoulders. "Just 'cause the company've never permitted it...."

"If a hunter's ever poached one, he never brought it to me to mount."

"Small wonder," Dowling said. "It'd take an eighteen-wheel flatbed to get it here."

"Too right," said the old man. "Though I remember, back in '53, one young bastard and his mates got the wobbly on and decided to sneak into the preserve and bag a tino. They stumbled upon a clutch of stralla eggs." He chuckled. "Then the stralla caught their scent. Those boys ran for their lives like jumbucks...."

The old man still chuckled as Dowling and Portia took their leave.

The third taxidermist's reception area had brighter sun-spectrum lights than the other two. A dusty minmi head stared down from above a mottled gray, synthetic stone counter. In a corner near the minmi's head, a smoke-brown wart covered a surveillance camera.

When Dowling tapped the bell on the counter, a man shuffled out of the work area. Silver hair, thin on top but brushing his shoulders. In Portia's hometown, she would have interpreted his hairstyle as that of a professional with a high-rise office taking up some rough-and-tumble hobby during a midlife crisis. She couldn't tell what it might mean around here. Certainly, no professional in an office would leave so much nostril hair in his turned-up nose.

With a booming yet guarded voice, the taxidermist asked, "How can I help ya?"

"Have a minute?" Dowling said. "I don't want to tie you up if you're busy."

"Nah, it's the slow season."

Portia briefly squinted at the man's clean workshirt. His cologne was as thick the others', but without any need for it. She inhaled quietly and caught only traces of chemicals from the work area out back. His season was slower than the others'.

"I'm down from Cookland," Dowling said, "scouting for a hunting trip coming up in three weeks. Looking for the lay of the land, meeting blokes I can work with, that sort of thing."

The silver-haired man's voice brightened. "You'll need taxidermy, then. What are you going after?"

"Dinos."

A quick nod. "I can do dinos."

"Good. Yeah, I was thinking about... winners."

The taxidermist blinked rapidly and his head jittered. He regained his composure, fixing wide eyes on Dowling and darting his head forward and back about five centimeters at a time.

The special agent dipped his chin in a single nod. With portentious ease he turned to Portia. "Be a love and turn off your neury."

She scowled at him while her thoughts raced. What would some superficial woman do? Like Tiana Spence, lunching yesterday with her and Portia's male boss. "I'm watching a very important story."

"Oh?"

"Princess Julia was seen at a gala in New Can last night. Her skirt was hemmed two centimeters above the knee." When Dowling said nothing, she said. "Above the knee! When we get home, you'll have to buy me an entire new wardrobe."

Dowling gave her a smile that reached his eyes, though she wished it hadn't. "Home is four thousand klicks away. Turn off your damned neury."

If he tired of law enforcement, he could find work as an actor playing villains. Her eyelids fluttered. She ducked her gaze. One last ping before she turned off her neury told her Dowling had powered down his too.

The taxidermist looked between the two of them. He licked his lips and nodded. "There's no microphone in here, but—" He rolled his eyes up and back, in the direction of the surveillance camera. "—watch that your lips might get read."

"I can talk like this," Dowling said. He didn't mumble but his lips barely moved. Forget acting, he could do ventriloquy. "And lovey's not going to say a word. Right, lovey?"

Portia swallowed thickly. Her head bobbed up and down.

The taxidermist's voice boomed. "You want a winner, you said?"

"Would that be a problem?"

"The dino company doesn't give winner permits."

Dowling's smile bared teeth. "I'm aware of that. If I need a winner mounted, would that be a problem?"

"No, no. Not at all. I've got a lot of experience—"

"With winners?" Dowling's voice dripped doubt.

The taxidermist opened his mouth, then leaned back. His eyes narrowed. "Are you johnny law? You have to tell me the truth, 'cause if you lie, the rest of this conversation is, what do they call it, in-trap-mint."

Dowling pivoted his head to Portia. "He's never done a winner. Come along, lovey. We'll figure this out another way." He turned his shoulders to face her, excluding the taxidermist.

"Good," Portia said. "I can get back to my video about Princess Julia."

The special agent laid a hand on her upper arm and directed her torso to turn toward the door. They each took a step—

"Wait," said the taxidermist. His words came out in a desperate flood. "You're right, mate, I've never mounted a winner. But I've done other dinos, how hard can it be? You wouldn't have to bring in a bloke from Port Bounty or nothing."

Dowling stopped. He turned his broad shoulders like an ocean-going cargo ship slowly changing bearing to enter the harbor at Endeavour Bay. "Which bloke?"

The taxidermist shook his head, as if flicking the question off the tip of his up-turned nose. "I'll charge a better price. Plus you don't have to pay for my flight down or a room to flop."

"Or a truck big enough to drive a winner's corpse here."

"Yeah, that too, mate, of course." The taxidermist grinned like a child hoping a strict parent would indulge him with candy.

"Plus," Dowling said, "Port Bounty's a big place. I wouldn't know where to look for him."

"And you can always find me here."

Dowling's baggy eyes regarded the silver-haired man. "I'll keep you in mind. G'day."

After the crunch of gravel gave way to the whisper of asphalt, a grin creased Dowling's face. "That makes a heck of a lot of sense, doesn't it? The suspect's got the devil's own pile of quid. He can hire the best taxidermist in Port Bounty."

"Or any of the bigger cities on Cookland," Portia said.

"You've the hang of this, doctor. Fly down the man and his supplies, put him up in a hotel.... So the taxidermist from the big smoke cools his heels at the hotel while the suspect sneaks onto the preserve, poaches a dino, and brings back the skin or as much of the carcass as will fit on a truck."

A limp bit of neck and sightless head of a winner draped across one of two queen beds in a bog standard room, with blood still dripping. " Not to the hotel."

"Ripper. Did he bring the taxidermist with him? Mount the skins in the field? How much equipment would the taxidermist need to bring with him?"

Portia shook her head. Her imagination suddenly flashed to the winner cow, shot through the chest, long neck collapsing.

Dowling went on. "Too much equipment and too much time to mount the skin out on the preserve. And you're right, he didn't do it in a hotel. The suspect must've set up his hired taxidermist in a building somewhere."

It was a small town, yet, "There must be quite a number of suitable buildings here in Blenheim," Portia said.

"And thousands of barns and sheds on farms between here and the preserve." The ute slowed and turned into the hotel's nearly empty parking lot. They parked near the front doors and climbed out. Bright globular streetlights at the corners of the lot cast X-shaped shadows on the asphalt.

An hour later, after they checked into their adjoining rooms and Portia unpacked and changed clothes, they met in the hotel's restaurant for a late lunch. A plush red rope blocked off a darkened half of the dining area. A solitary waiter, a stiff-backed boy fresh out of school, with more acne than whiskers on his face, took their orders, then returned with their two cups of tea.

"I did some research into taxidermy just now," Portia said. "You're right, it couldn't have been performed on site. There's too much equipment to feasibly drive onto the preserve. Chemicals to clean the skins, wire and foam to construct a mannequin, and the tools to work those materials. And even with modern tech, the process takes at least a day, and more like three or four if the taxidermist wants his work to qualify as a handicraft." She poured sweetened milk in her tea and sipped.

"We could go knock on five thousand doors looking for their worksite," Dowling said. "That obviously won't go."

"I trust you're thinking aloud," Portia asked. "I'm not a policewoman."

Dowling chuckled. "That's how I work. Like a scientist. I kick around hypotheses that fit what we know, then do research to test them."

Portia raised her eyebrows. Her image of frontos had the square-jawed, but somewhat dim, heroes of cartoons and action movies baked in. "You're not what I expected from a Frontier Policeman."

"And how many frontos have you ever met, doctor?" He spoke lightly.

She reached for her tea to mask a warmth on her cheeks and give her gaze an excuse to drop from his eyes. Though she was no more than ten standard years younger than him, she felt like a naïve girl.

The special agent's voice took on a down-to-business tone. "We need more leads. I called our regional office in Port Bounty and head-quarters in New Can, to see if any prominent taxidermists have made repeated trips down here. I also enquired about any real estate the suspect or his family might own in the area. No word yet."

Portia sipped more from her cuppa. "I don't want to wait around the hotel till they get back to you."

"We won't. But why don't you want to wait?"

The squeak of the waiter's trainers on the hardwood floor heralded the arrival of their lunch. For her, hydroponic greens and cherry toma-toes strewn with slices of seared tuna and drizzled with a balsamic vinaigrette. She knifed greens and a protein slice into a dainty bite, and hesitated with the fork near her mouth. If she weren't careful talking about her feelings, she'd make herself sick. "Martinson needs to be punished for what he did."

Dowling swallowed a mouthful of cheeseburger. "You're a loyal employee," he said.

She could tell from his voice that he intentionally said something he didn't believe, but she couldn't stop herself from speaking harshly. "I'm not angry for the company's interests. I'm angry about those dinos he slaughtered."

"You don't like hunting."

Portia jammed the forkful of salad into her mouth. She chewed vigorously, glad to have an excuse to delay her answer. After swallow-ing, she said, "I don't like killing anything, especially the dinos, but I know there's a purpose for it. Managing herd numbers to stay within carrying capacity, balancing our interests against those of our neigh-bors...." She squeezed her eyes shut for a moment, drew a breath. "Hunting's part of the circle of life. But what he did? He knew he had no right to shoot the winner and every other dino he poached and he did it anyway." She hissed out the final words.

Sometime while she spoke, Dowling had rested his cheeseburger on his plate. He regarded her with his baggy eyes. "You've got a lot of fire in your belly for this case. That's good. But keep it under control."

"Why?" she asked. Her sharp tone of voice wasn't like her at all. She took a breath and said, much more properly, "Oh, for evidence and police procedure reasons."

"Those too."

She blinked. "What am I missing, special agent?"

"When you kick over rocks, you never know when you'll surprise a venomous snake."

Portia pulled her arms closer to her ribs. "The suspect is in custody, isn't he?"

"His father bailed him out. The judge ordered him to remain in Port Bounty or the neighboring shire. But I'm not talking about the suspect or the taxidermist. The suspect had local help. Someone provided him the bulldozer to bury the winner's corpse, right? Others might have been involved, too."

"If we find the local help, they might turn violent? Why?"

"Ten counts of dinosaur poaching could be punished with a sizable amount of personality modification and a fine that would garnish half a workingman's wages for a century. And a man who breaks one law tends to break others. The punishment for all his crimes might go well beyond what he's already facing. Escaping that might in his mind justify violence. And a man living a life of crime tends to act impulsively to begin with."

"I'll be careful."

"Good," Dowling said with a trace of affection.

Portia's head snapped up. Did he harbor an attraction for her? The look in his baggy eyes and the outdated style of his jacket showed otherwise. Affectionate like an uncle, not an aspiring boyfriend.

Muscles in her face eased. The greens and reds on her plate made her want to wolf them down. "What, then, is our plan for the rest of the day?"

"We find the building where Lachlan Martinson set up the taxidermist."

Her eyebrows rose. "We'll knock on five thousand doors?"

Dowling laughed. "No. Just one."

3

———

The real estate agent's office filled the front half of the middle floor of a five-story building in downtown Blenheim. A planter box crowded with greenery ran the width of the room, in front of floor-to-ceiling windows behind her desk. Leafy and earthy smells, moist from drip irrigation, filled the room. The windows faced across the street the shire council office, a building crowned with stone towers topped with finials. Too massive a building for its city block. Beyond the council office, light glowed on the northwestern horizon.

Portia frowned. Too bright to be winter twilight this far south. She pointed. "What's all that?"

The real estate agent looked that way and blinked eyes with long lashes. Vanessa Wilford, said the name laser-etched on the glass door. She spoke with a voice that tried to be chummy but failed. "That's the ancient British history museum." Portia had lived in Port Bounty long enough to recognize her accent as being from that city.

Dowling acted the part of the crass rich man. "This town's a hell of an odd place for one."

A naughty thrill ran through Portia at the swear word. *Wait, you're* *pretending to be a rich man's kept woman, and your knickers are in a twist over **hell**?*

"Blenheim is named after the ancestral estate of some names you might have heard of." Wilford ticked them off on long fingers. "The Duke of Marlborough, Winston Churchill, Princess Diana. And the museum's symbolic of why I, and many others, have moved here. Sit, please. Tea?"

"I'll take a cuppa," Portia said.

Dowling shook his head, lips pursed. "Which is?"

The real estate agent pressed the buttons on the billy. Hot steam carried the scent of Earl Grey to Portia's nose.

Wilford turned back to Dowling. "Opportunity. My husband and I moved down in '64."

Portia blinked. From the woman's wavy black hair and the dusting of freckles on her smooth cheeks, all seen under the sharp glare of sun-spectrum ceiling panels, she'd guessed the real estate agent to be two decades younger.

"The town might have had five hundred residents, all living within a few blocks of the original council office." Wilford waved long fingers toward the window. "But we knew the dinosaur preserve would bring in tourists, and tourists would inspire people to further development, like the museum. More development would mean more jobs, would mean high wages to attract workers from up north, would mean high demand for real estate."

Dowling said, "I take it you've done well enough to justify leaving Port Bounty all those years ago."

"Well enough." Wilford handed Portia a recyclable cup, then sat behind her desk. She swiveled her chair to face Dowling. "How can I help you?"

"I'm looking to buy a country getaway. Someplace secluded, between here and the dino preserve. We'd come down during the summer and rent out the land to a riddlepig farmer or—"

"Pigs?" On cue, Portia wrinkled her nose. "Don't they put up a horrid stink?"

Dowling gave her an indulgent smile masking a sharp edge. "You paying any quid for this, lovey?"

With a quiet clearing of her throat, Wilford brought their attention back to her. "More and more sophisticated people are discovering the quiet joys of a country getaway. We have a good number of properties that could meet your needs."

"I knew Lackey gave us a dinkum reco."

A smile pushed up the freckles on Wilford's cheeks, though confusion touched her eyes. "Word of mouth is the best advert," she said, "but which 'Lackey' do you mean?"

Portia's heart pounded. They were taking a flyer, that Martinson had sought out the one real estate agent in town whose public bio spoke of growing up in Port Bounty, when he needed to find a base for his poaching.

"Lachlan Martinson," Dowling said. "He's a young bloke from Port Bounty. I met him a few years back, at a hunting lodge in the north Cookland bush."

Wilford's mouth quirked at the name before she forced her smile wider. "Of course. I went to secondary school with his father."

"You helped him find a 'country place,' but I couldn't tell if he meant a farm spread or a place in town."

"A farm. Very much like what you want, except he wanted a rental rather than a place for sale. A good way out of town. The back paddocks border the dino preserve."

Portia's breath caught. She clawed her way back into character and rolled her eyes. "I suppose dinos stink less than riddlepigs."

"She's telling us what Lackey got, lovey, not what I want." He angled his head and one eyebrow crept up. "Not necessarily." To Wilford, he said, "You have the address?"

Portia stamped her foot. "You *cannot* be serious. Bad enough you only want to be seen in public with me in a woop woop town thousands of klicks from anyone who might know you have a—"

"Lovey." Dowling's voice knifed through the room.

Portia quailed. On the other hand, after Wilford returned her attention from her neury, she gave the special agent a look of cougarish appraisal. With a husk in her voice, she said, "21 Shire Road 79-58."

"Half an hour in our ute?"

"Closer to an hour. The farm is on a gravel road over twenty klicks east of the main highway to the dino preserve."

"We'll run by on our way to check out some other properties you might be able to give us."

"Of course. I have a good number of places that might fit your needs. It will help if you give me a price range."

With a wince in his baggy eyes, the special agent said, "I can't go too high. What would a million quid get me?"

Wilford blinked at Dowling, then swept black hair behind her ear with her long fingers. "You'll be spoiled for choice...."

Portia and Special Agent Dowling left the real estate office twenty minutes later, with a list of five properties located between Blenheim and the preserve. Wilford offered to ride out with them, saying to Dowling while ignoring Portia, "My husband and I've no plans for the evening, he won't mind if I show you."

"We'll take a look around on our own, then get back in touch when we're ready to make an offer on one." Dowling put on a courteous smile which stayed on his face until the ute pulled up to the curb and they climbed in. The leather of the rear seats crinkled under her. Dowling sat opposite her, at the front of the cabin, facing the rear. The doors thumped shut before he said, "I wouldn't want to be the unlucky bastard married to her."

"I thought a woman her age would have outgrown the urge to flirt."

Dowling chortled. "The wonders of modern medicine. Never mind that. We've got a lead."

"Your hunch panned out."

"I figured Martinson would want to play things close to the vest. Shire Road 79-58, here we come."

The ute worked its way through downtown Blenheim and to the main southbound road. Cars and other utes crowded the road near fish-and-chips and pizza takeaways, pubs, and a city park with a well-lit footy pitch.

Why so much traffic? She checked the time through her neury and blinked in surprise. Already twenty-four o'clock, the end of the workday. Between their late lunch and the lack of even an hour of twilight, she'd lost track of time.

Which ticked by as the ute hummed its way down the asphalt two-lane, into the even deeper darkness of the south polar winter evening. The town and its glowing lights thinned out. Side roads branched off on both sides. Wide, asphalted, and frequent at first, by ten klicks south of Blenheim, the side roads were gravel gouges a lane-and-a-half wide, running due east-west, hitting the highway about two klicks apart. Only the signs posting them as shire roads made them seem anything more than farmers' driveways.

Between the side roads, fences ran along the two-lane. The only turnouts led to farmhouses set a thousand meters off the road, or wireless comms towers.

When the ute passed Shire Road 79-54, the numbering suddenly made sense. "That's latitude, isn't it? 79°54' south?"

"You've got it. Don't drive around here much?"

"We get around in quaddies, usually."

Dowling said nothing, but Portia suddenly felt spoiled. She lowered her gaze a moment. "You frontos spend a lot of time in ground vehicles?"

"Yeah, but I also know the region I'm working."

"I've only been with the company three local years!" She hugged her arms to her sides. "You needn't be judgmental."

"I wasn't," Dowling said mildly. "Should I've been? Are you one of those?"

"One of those what?"

"A city slicker who thinks the millions of data shufflers in the big smoke matter and rural folk in woop woop towns don't?"

Portia felt chill. She managed to say, "I only called Blenheim a woop woop town to stay in character..."

Dowling raised his hand, palm-out. "You did well. And I want you to remember something. To the folk around here, the corner of Dinosaur Preserve Highway and Shire Road 79-58 is as important as the corner of Coronation and Bourke in downtown Endeavour Bay."

She'd been there. After graduation, she'd taken the tube downtown with her parents for dinner at a ninetieth-floor restaurant looking out on the rippling bay. To get to the restaurant from the tube station, they'd walked crowded sidewalks and crossed the street at the most famous intersection on the planet. Thousands of footsteps, thousands of electric car motors humming, all echoing down urban canyons walled with steel, glass, and carbon nanotube alloys. Unease had tempered her jubilant mood. One young woman in one large city. Would real life fulfill all her dreams from uni?

The young women, and young men, and the children, the middle-aged, the elderly of both sexes from around here had dreams too, and the challenge to fulfill them.

"Thank you. I hadn't thought of that."

"Come to think of it, I want you to remember something else. When your dad gets his new, cloned liver out of a riddlepig, or your mum one-ups the rest of her bridge club by bringing a bottle of the trendiest new syrah, they can do those things because of rural folk in woop woop towns."

"My dad doesn't drink that much...." That wasn't the point. "I shouldn't take the people around here for granted."

Dowling grinned. "I'll make a fronta of you yet, Dr. Oakeshott." The ute slowed. The special agent craned his neck. "I reckon here's our turn."

The ute's headlights swept over the sign for Shire Road 79-58. Gravel rattled under the wheels. Washboard ripples shook the ute. Ahead, the gravel road ran straight, up and down rolls in the terrain, as far as the headlights could illuminate. Farmhouses and comms towers stood in dark fields. Barbed-wire fences flanked the road. Behind them grazed riddlepigs, sheep sheared for natural wool, ranches of free-range cattle, hunting parks stocked with emus. More than she had imagined.

Something else came to mind. "The farm rented by Lachlan Martinson is on this road? And its back fence is at the outer perimeter of the dinosaur preserve?"

"Both."

The crown grant of land for the preserve began at 80° south. A minute of latitude on New New South Wales was about one kilometer. "The farm is two klicks from front to back?"

"And two wide. Standard for this area."

"We'll have to go on site to investigate."

"Eventually, yes. First we'll drive by. We can do that without a warrant."

The ute rolled on. A combination of washboarded road and the crest of a terrain roll jostled her so hard the seatbelt tensed, the shoulder strap too tight across her chest. By the time she unbuckled and rebuckled with a little slack, Dowling's head lolled back. He breathed slowly and his baggy eyes were closed.

When you get a chance to sleep, take it. *Wake me five minutes before we get to Number 21*, she told her neury. After one last look at the dark farmland on both sides of the ute, she shut her eyes, doubting she'd fall asleep.

A glow inside her eyelids and a bonging in her ears roused her. Her neury told her the ute approached Number 19, the farm adjacent their target. Narrow steel fenceposts, each painted white and one-meter-fifty tall, lined the roadside like soldiers at attention. Taut barbed wire stretched between them. Portia expected black or gray cattle to be grazing in the field behind the fences, but she couldn't see them in the polar gloom.

The barbed wire fence curved away from the roadside at the entrance to a narrow gravel lane. No gate, just a set of pipes running laterally across the top of a trench the width of the lane. During her livestock training, she'd learned the pipe-and-trench structure was called a cattle guard.

A sign rising up from the last fencepost before the curve bore red paint artistically announcing *One Family Under God—The Yeardleys*. Five meters behind and to the far side of the gate rose a plain white cross, six or eight meters tall and gleaming in the glow of ground-mounted floodlights.

Dowling blinked at the giant cross, then bowed his head to Portia. "Now that's a wowser. I'll never call you one again."

He reached into his jacket and pulled out an object barely larger than the last joint of his thumb. His trimmed fingernails pried at something. In the dim light, his baggy eyes scowled. "I'm not having luck. You have a go, doctor."

The special agent extended his arms. Into her palm he dropped the object. A black plastic disc, two centimeters in diameter and one thick.

A white strip ringed the disc near the circumference on one side. "A go at...?"

"The adhesive backing."

A pair of glassy circles stared out of the disc. Camera lenses. "Ah." Portia worked her fingernail into a seam in the backing and peeled it off. She cradled it in her fingers, sticky- and camera-side up, and handed it back.

Dowling took it, twisted in his seat, and pressed it to a lower corner of the ute's side window. Portia could barely see it next to the health and safety stickers she hadn't noticed.

"I'll share the camera feed to your neury," Dowling said.

"How much can a camera see in the dark?"

"A good bit. Night vision. Image processing."

She accessed the camera. Her neury showed her a greenish augmented reality overlay on her view out the window. Distant dots, glowing on four legs, were the Yeardley's cattle.

The ute rolled on. A minute after passing the Yeardleys' front gate, the straight white fenceposts were replaced by thicker ones, two meters tall, of unpainted steel. A helix of razor wire crested the top of the new fence, angled in.

She shivered. No family farm, this. That fence could better keep out a boomer, a full-grown male kangaroo... except the razor wire coil aimed to keep something *in*. But Dowling's camera showed only rolling ground tufted with unkempt grasses, with no animal visible. In the distance, a grove of trees covered a low ridge. Her neury estimated the range to the grove at fifteen hundred meters.

"The whole back paddock is out of sight from the road," Dowling said.

The ute soon came to the entrance to Number 21. No cattle guard. Instead, a powered gate of unpainted metal flashed past. About eight hundred meters behind the gate, two pole-mounted lights glowed. One over the front yard of a one-story rambler house clad in slabs of native limestone, the other over the closed carriage doors of a sheet metal barn.

Gravel rumbled under the tires. The razor wire fence passed monotonously by.

"The taxidermist should have had plenty of room in that barn to work," Portia said.

Dowling sucked air through his teeth. "We still haven't proven anything. Let's take a squizz at the sat imagery."

Portia's neury overlaid an aerial still image onto her view of the left-hand window. A summery patchwork of greens lay between a narrow beige strip and a zone of deeper, splotchier green. The deeper green meant cycads and ferns foresting the dino preserve. Shadows stretching from some of the green patches and splotches indicated groves of trees. Other shadows flowed from contours of the land. Two squared-off shadows marked the house and barn.

"Bugger. The image is too old. Taken before Martinson rented the farm. But it can still tell us some things." He swept his fingertip over a green patch and the edge of a shadowed zone. "This is the grove and the ridge we saw from the road." His fingertip circled the full zone of shadow and a sunlit area between the shadow and the dino preserve. "I wonder if you can see this area from the neighboring farms."

His finger tapped air. The image zoomed in on the fence near the front corner shared with the Yeardleys. With a smile in his voice, Dowling said, "You little ripper!"

"What do you see?"

"Check the fencepost shadows between the two farms."

After a moment, Portia's eyebrows lifted. "They're the same lengths."

"Which means?"

"Martinson had the tall razor wire fence built."

"Highly likely... but still not proof."

The ute approached the lane of the next farm. "Chuck a yewy here," Dowling told the vehicle. It slowed and made a three-point turn. A brief respite from the rattle of the ute along the gravel road.

"Back to Blenheim?" Portia asked.

The ute picked up speed. The augmented reality view of farmland to the right vanished in a blink.

Dowling tugged the camera off the window. "Not yet. We've seen all we can from the road. But I reckon the Yeardleys might let us take a squizz from another angle."

4

The Yeardleys' house, a two-story bungalow of honey-colored bricks and an umber-red metal roof rippled to look like spanish tile, sat primly and properly at the crest of a gentle rise. A veranda running the full front of the house held rocking chairs, a loveseat on a porch swing, and a small wicker table. Small flowerbeds under shining growlights dotted the broad front lawn and ringed the bases of oaks with roses and lilies.

As a girl, Portia had played with fairy dolls in her mum's flowerbeds, much like these.... but the calligraphed signs jutting up from the mulched soil, quoting Bible verses with extra flourishes on the capital letters in *Lord* and *God*, suggested that fairy dolls had best land elsewhere.

Dowling led the way across the lawn on a concrete footpath. The scent of fresh-cut grass mingled with the earthiness of the flowerbeds. Oak branches reached for each other overhead, like the loving elderly couple transformed into trees in some myth from ancient ancient Greece.

Pagan myths might be unwelcome here, too.

Lights snapped on at the edge of the veranda's roof. The spring of a storm door twanged and Portia squinted at the front door of the house.

A matronly figure stepped onto the veranda. A loose-fitting dress covered her from neck to wrists and ankles. "G'day."

Dowling's footsteps scraped to a halt on the concrete. He looked up and inclined his head a few centimeters. "G'day. I'm Special Agent Dowling, Frontier Police." He flashed his badge, then gestured palm-up toward Portia. "This is Do—Miss Oakeshott."

Portia bowed. She put on a smile her grandmother would be proud of. "G'day. Mrs. Yeardley?"

"Yes." Mrs. Yeardley pivoted her gaze to Dowling. Portia couldn't place her lilting accent. "Frontier Police? Is something the matter?"

"Not here. Your farm is a lovely spread. Places like this make me excited to go to the office every morning."

Portia's vision adapted well enough to make out Mrs. Yeardley's demure smile. "We strive to always do what is pleasing in the sight of the Lord." The smile faded. "Something is the matter elsewhere?"

Dowling's face looked pained. He angled his head in the direction of Martinson's farm.

Mrs. Yeardley wrung her hands, then gestured at the rocking chairs and porch swing. "Come on up, have a seat. I'll ask my husband to join us. Would you care for tea? A caf? A soft drink?"

Portia and the special agent made their requests. Another twang of the storm door's spring. They waited on the veranda while the muffled voices and pounding footsteps of children drifted to them from inside the house. The floodlights aimed at the yard turned off, sending the veranda into a cool but comfortable semi-darkness lit only by lamps inside the house diffused by lace curtains across the windows.

Mrs. Yeardley emerged five minutes later with a steel tray bearing drinks. With her came a man with black hair receding from the sides of his forehead. He raised a thick arm bulging against the unwrinkled sleeve of a flannel shirt. "G'day, special agent, I'm Mick Yeardley," he said in a gravelly voice as he shook Dowling's hand. Portia couldn't place his accent, either.

"Please, sit," Mrs. Yeardley added.

Dowling took one of the rocking chairs, Portia the other. Mrs. Yeardley handed out drinks, then joined her husband on the porch swing. The warmth of Portia's steaming cuppa softened the cool of the evening. Giggles sounded from just the other side of the wall.

"The missus says you're here about our neighbor?" asked Yeardley.

"Yes. First, what can you tell us about him?"

"Well, we never see the bloke. He lives up Port Bounty most of the time but you prolly know that. We can tell he's in if the lights are on at the house or we see cars up and down the road."

"What times is he about?" Dowling asked.

"Winters. Three or four days at a stretch." THe storm door's spring squeaked. Without turning his head, Yeardley said, voice firm, "You lot need to go to bed. We have to get up at one o'clock to make it to church, remember?"

Portia shivered and pulled her tea cup closer to her body. Twenty-four-sevens. They'd be offended if you called them that. Church of Christ Risen on the First Day. Fanatics who kept their church calendar by Earth's, instead of the thirty-four-hour days and seven or eight day weeks of New New South Wales. Portia had heard of the denomination, but had never met an adherent growing up in Esperance Heights' leafy suburban streets.

"Children," Yeardley said, his voice honed to sharper edge.

Portia craned her neck. A boy of perhaps five standard and a girl a couple of standard years older, both with cheeky looks on their faces, darted back from the storm door, trailing giggles.

"Go on, you heard Dad," a teenaged boy called after them. His voice warbled. He peered out the open door. A gangly build, dark brown hair slicked against his scalp, acne splotching his face. Portia remembered awkward boys at school dances. His brown-eyed gaze met hers and grew puzzled. "Are you a fronto?"

Dowling leaned forward. "Yes."

Yeardley swiveled and fixed the boy with a gimlet eye. "It's not just the young ones who need to go to bed."

The boy's brown eyes turned down. "Yes, Dad."

Yeardley's mouth quirked. "They're good sprats, most of the time."

"We regret the inconvenience," said Dowling. "We didn't know they had an early bedtime today."

"No, no. I'm glad Martinson ended up on your radar "

Portia's head made a half-turn before she could think. Had a shadow crossed the curtained window behind her? She blinked and sipped tea. Maybe she was seeing things.

Yeardley showed no sign of noticing anything either. To his wife, he said, "Beloved, be a helpmeet and get the kids to bed."

"Gladly." Mrs. Yeardley stood up, set down her fizzing cola on the side table. Her husband took her arms and pulled her down for a kiss. She walked toward the front door with a pleased smile on her face.

After the screen door twanged behind her, Yeardley planted his foot and brought the porch swing to a stop. "I don't think she could add anything to what I can tell you, and I'd rather we not talk about it in front of her."

Dowling scooted forward. The back ends of his chair's rockers poked into the air like bony spikes on a *Kunbarrasaurus'* tail. "What can you tell us?"

"As we said, we can sometimes see cars heading up Martinson's lane. I was working the side paddock late one winter night, this was, two local years ago? Yeah, two. One of the heifers was about to drop her first calf and she wandered off and," Yeardley drew a breath, "a team of frontos don't need to hear about a farmer's troubles."

Dowling nodded. "You were in the side paddock?"

"Yeah, it was, oh bugger, two or three o'clock. I was on a gentle rise and could see the full thousand meters to Martinson's lane and house. A car rolls up and out come three, ah...." Yeardley avoided Portia's gaze.

"You can't offend me," she said, feeling a naughty thrill as she fibbed to the man. "I've worked vice."

Dowling coughed. He raised an eyebrow at her. The farmer wasn't watching her, so she winked back.

Yeardley thickly swallowed. In the dim light, Portia couldn't tell if her words made him blush. "Yes," he said, "three of them, and their attire and demeanor left no doubt how they came by their quid."

"I see," Dowling said. "Thank you. Our investigation had not yet turned up any evidence of, ah, white slavery."

"I'm glad I brought it to your attention, then. We're good people, not just those of who believe He rose on the first day, but almost everyone around here. We don't want that element getting a foothold."

"We understand," Portia said. She sneaked a glance at Dowling. Couldn't he get the farmer on point?

The special agent extended his hand toward her, palm down, and dribbled air like a basketball. All the while he kept his gaze on Yeardley. "We knew a girl disappeared but we didn't know she worked in that trade."

"Disappeared?"

"No one talks about the missing girl?"

"We don't talk about women of ill repute, whether live or dead." Yeardley raised an insulated metal cup of tea to his mouth, but didn't sip. "Though she is a child of God, no matter how far she wandered from the Good Shepherd's flock."

Dowling paused. "Do you know something?"

"From time to time we hear gunshots from Martinson's place. Enough to get dinos on the preserve bellowing like a bull trying to get to a cow in heat. We can't see where Martinson's shooting from or what he's shooting at, but it sounds like they come from his back paddock." Yeardley waved in the direction of the wooded slope on Martinson's farm. "Could he have...?"

"It's possible," Dowling said.

"And sometimes clanking sounds. I thought of earth-moving equipment. Dear God." From the sound of Yeardley's voice, Portia guessed his face had drained of blood.

Dowling said, "I know you're a good family man and you have to wake up at one o'clock for church the same as your wife and children. Would you grant us permission to recon his farm from your side paddock? When we're done, we'll drive off without needing to bother you."

"What do you think you can find?"

"We don't know. We want to gather as much evidence as we can to maximize the chance the judge approves the search warrant."

Yeardley huffed out a breath. "Search warrants. The Americans collapsed because they rejected God, and we emulate their ways."

"I hear you," Dowling said. Amazing how his tone of voice could imply agreement when his words were noncommital. "But officially, we're limited to saying, make those wishes known to your MP."

Yeardley nodded. "The side paddocks are fallow. We keep the cattle close to the hay barn during the dark weeks. God bless you both."

All rose and shook hands. Dowling led the way off the veranda and across dormant grass. They rounded the corner of the house and into a cool breeze from the south. He walked through a rectangle of light thrown onto the lawn from an upstairs window. A line crossed the rectangle near the house and the light slowly rippled. Portia glanced up. A window open a crack. Throw on a blankey for good sleeping weather.

"What do you think we'll see?" she asked.

The special agent grunted. His feet left soft grass for the crunch of the gravel lane.

The lane ended at a sheet metal barn with a pitched roof. The smell of hay lightly touched Portia's nose. Behind the barn, a cattlebeast mooed in sleepy contentment.

Light from the house dimmed with distance. A glance back showed Portia the upstairs window had gone dark. Gloom shrouded the ground and turned the barn ghostly gray. She glanced up at the stars. That red dot was Stella Australis B, the lesser star in their binary system. She remembered as a child marveling at stories and pictures of the moon of far-off Earth.

Dowling pulled a flashlight from his inner pocket. He hooked a curled piece around his ear and turned on the light. When he glanced down, a pallid circle a meter across lit up the ground. Enough illumination to see a hole before one twisted an ankle in it.

They came to a slatted metal gate one-meter-fifty high and wide enough for a ute. Dowling glanced at the chain binding it to a post, then at Portia. "You up for a climb?" He didn't wait for a reply. Instead he went up the slats like a ladder, swung his legs over the top, and jumped backward to the ground on the far side.

Her arms moved freely in her jacket. Dowling led her feet with the light as she did the same.

They were in a paddock, yet with fences so small and distant she imagined walking across an open prairie. Tufted grass swatted at her shins. Crickets jumped whizzing along the ground. The special agent veered his path around crumbly brown chips of dried cow manure.

Portia trudged on. The image of the winner cow's mounted head came to the inside of her eyelids when she blinked. What evidence might they find that would do right by her?

"If Yeardley didn't see anything from his side paddock," she said, "what makes you think you will?"

"We don't have to *see* anything, doctor," said Dowling over his shoulder. He stopped walking. "Come to think of it, here's as good a place to calibrate the sniffer as any." He reached into his jacket.

"How many pockets do you have in your jacket?"

"Enough." His voice revealed he grinned. He brought out an object and glanced down to his hand. The flashlight over his ear bathed the object in light.

A gray plastic cube, tiny against his palm, with a funnel as long as the cube's main body jutting from a side. A molded plastic ring flanged off the opposite side. He tapped a button on another side, or was the entire side the button? A fan whined at high speed. LEDs cycled yellow, then green.

He clipped the molded plastic ring to a carabiner on his jacket. "I'll share you the baseline," the special agent said.

Portia's neury popped text over her vision where the dark, rolling field met the star-crusted sky.

Cadaverine < 1 ppm

Putrescine < 1 ppm

Geosmin < 5 ppm

and other compounds she didn't immediately recognize. She didn't need to. Her nose wrinkled at a memory of the first two compounds in a training lab. Unmistakable indicators of rotting flesh. The third compound was the scent of freshly-dug earth.

Which meant... "You think Martinson buried the dinos near the preserve's perimeter?"

The cool breeze rustled the leaves of a dozen sweetgum trees. "There's a chance they're buried on the farm. That gives him a defense that they wandered off the preserve and were fair game."

A hundred meters farther, a trickle came to her ears. A jagged gash across the ground twenty meters ahead had to be a gully with flowing water. Dowling's flashlight panned across a patch of bare dirt gouging out the gully wall. Cattle hooves had cratered the patch. Portia waved her arms for balance and the special agent aimed his beam at the ground in front of her.

After they hopped the trickling watercourse and scrambled up the gully's far bank, Portia said, "That can't be it. Mr. Pietrangelo said surveillance video showed no dinos crossed the perimeter—what?"

Dowling grabbed her forearm. He peered into the gloom, in the direction of the sweetgums. In a harsh whisper, he asked, "You hear anything?"

Portia angled her head and cupped her hand behind her ear. "No," she murmured.

"All those days and weeks crossing the system in tin cans, I lost some hearing. Let's keep moving." He led her across the field, in the direction of the wooded ridge hiding Martinson's back paddock from sight.

She checked the numbers from the special agent's sniffer.

Cadaverine 2 ppm

Putrescine 3 ppm

Geosmin 7 ppm

Random fluctuations? Plenty of things died on a farm, and a wild animal digging a burrow could kick up some fresh earth.

"Back to what you were saying," the special agent said. "I hate to have to tell you, but regardless where he shot the dinos or buried them, Martinson had help from an employee of your company."

Portia vigorously shook her head, certain he could hear her gesture in the gloom. "He could have stolen the keys to earth-moving equipment. Especially if he's active in winter."

"Or he hired someone in company security to lose the audio and video of him herding a dino across the perimeter."

They came to a barbed-wire fence separating two paddocks of the Yeardleys' farm. While Dowling clambered easily over, she rolled her lips together. Company employees helping the poacher? Her stomach soured. "Good Lord, I hope you're wrong."

He shone the flashlight on the fence and gave her a hand. Enough space separated the barbs for her to put hands and feet on the strands. She pulled her arms in but still her jacket snagged on the top wire. Dowling helped her work the jacket loose with one hand while his other held her forearm. The taut wires wobbled like a high-wire act at a circus. She reached the ground without shredding her jacket.

Country life was not for her.

They continued across the paddock. Her neury's compass showed they headed southeast. The terrain rolled but generally fell to a grove of trees looming ahead in the starlight. Branches rustled in the breeze. An owl hooted and some small creature darted into undergrowth as Portia and the special agent entered the grove.

Dowling's hand rasped over a trunk. "Oaks."

She remembered gnarled branches swooping low enough to her back lawn for her seven-year-old self to sit on one while her bare toes brushed the ground. Here amid these oaks, the air seemed a trifle warmer and the musty smell of fallen leaves came pleasantly to her nose.

Something metallic glimmered between trees a dozen meters away. Portia gave a double-take, then let out a breath. One of the tall fence-posts of Martinson's farm.

Dowling wound his way through the trees. He stopped next to the fencepost and slapped his hand onto it. It rang faintly, unnatural in the winter night.

Cadaverine 5 ppm

Putrescine 8 ppm

Geosmin 17 ppm

Dowling looked past the fencepost. Barbed wire gleamed in the flashlight glow. Barbs sharper and more hooked than the ones between the Yeardleys' paddocks. Somewhere behind her, another small creature ran through the brush as if it too fled this monstrous fence. She hugged her arms against her torso.

The flashlight swept on, toward the ridgeline hiding Martinson's back paddock. The dark ground and immense vault of sky swallowed the flashlight beam.

What else had the ground swallowed?

The special agent's voice broke the night with a tone of pleased righteousness. "The decay and earth-moving molecules getting more prevalent the closer we get to the farm, plus Yeardley's statement about gunshots, bellowing dinos, and earth-moving equipment, add that to the grotesqueries in Martinson's basement in Port Bounty, and the judge will sign off on a warrant."

A fallen twig snapped three or four meters behind them. A young male voice warbled, "No he won't."

5

Portia's head snapped around. Next to an oak about four meters away, the beam of Dowling's flashlight threw a weak glow on the Yeardleys' teenage son.

And the rifle he held diagonally across his chest.

"Hands where I can see them," the boy said.

Dowling slowly spread his arms. He spoke slowly, casually, "What's all this about, mate?"

How? Portia's legs felt immobile, like concrete pillars sunk into the earth. Yet she wanted to run. Fast as she could.

The boy shifted his hands. Light danced along the rifle's front sight and the end of the barrel. The muzzle was the jet-black iris of a one-eyed carrion god.

With more warble in his voice, the boy said, "You know too much."

"Mate. Don't be the devil's own fool. I'm a fronto. My neury sends my location to headquarters round the clock. Even way out here at the bottom of the world. If something happens to Dr. Oakeshott or me, a paramilitary team will descend on our last known location. You'd be punished to the fullest extent of the law."

The boy angled the rifle's muzzle closer to Portia and the special agent. His eyes looked lifeless inside the grim mask of his face.

Portia's cheeks turned clammy as a corpse's. All Dowling had were words. The boy had a rifle and she couldn't move her legs to run and if she did the boy'd put a bullet through her back or blow a hole in her skull.

"And," Dowling said, "you'd break your Mum's heart."

The boy's face turned slack. His chest heaved with a breath. He pivoted the rifle, butt toward the ground, muzzle toward the underside of his chin—

"Bloody hell!" Dowling sprinted like a footy tagger out to tackle a ball carrier. But instead of wrapping his arms around the boy, he grabbed the rifle barrel at a full passing run and yanked the teenager off-balance.

The rifle roared in the night. The special agent and the boy tumbled amid the roots of oaks as birds squawked and beat their wings.

Portia unfroze in an instant. Ears ringing, she ran forward, aiming for the wobbling circle of illumination from Dowling's flashlight. The special agent flung the rifle away. It clattered into the darkness.

She kneeled beside Dowling. "Are you hurt?"

"What?" He squinted and massaged his ear with one hand. The look on his face showed he only guessed at her words. "I'm tinny."

Unhurt. Thank God. And the boy? He lay on the ground, his dark brown hair an unruly mess. He breathed rapidly and his eyes were squeezed shut.

Shock? She checked his pulse with fingertips at his neck while counting breaths. No sight nor smell of blood.

Also unhurt. Thank God for that, too.

The boy's hand fluttered up to his neck. His fingers clamped on her hand. His whole arm shook. "Almighty God what I have I done Almighty God."

"There there." Portia could think of nothing more to say.

"Oh God Almighty God I've already broken her heart."

If you were a mother? If he were your boy? "No. She'll forgive you. He who Rose on the First Day will forgive you. But you've got to tell us everything they'll forgive you for."

Dowling gave her a grin, like a geiersaur preparing to wolf down fresh kill. She raised her eyebrows and hardened her jaw. A moment later he lowered his abashed gaze to the boy's face.

The boy's arm stilled. His crushing grip on Portia's hand eased. "I will."

"Can you sit up?"

He nodded and let go of her hand. With a wince, he pushed himself up on his elbows, then scooted on his rump to put his back against the nearest oak. His breaths slowed. He avoided their eyes.

"When Martinson rented the place, he needed workers to put up the new fence. Local boys. Dad said good on ya, sweat like a man in the summer sun and earn some money, just as long as you keep Sunday as the Sabbath. I was nervous as can be. Fourteen standard, and Martinson was this laired-up rich bloke all the way from *Port Bounty*. But instead of mocking me as a twenty-four-sevener, he brought me in on the joke. We'd be mates and tell Dad and Mum what they wanted to hear." He thumped the back of his head against the tree trunk. "Mum."

Dowling opened his mouth. Portia extended her hand to him and spoke instead. "Tell us more about Martinson, if you would."

"So we're building the fence and I work up the nerve to ask why it's so bloody high. Why the razor wire on top angles in. Why he built a gate at the back boundary with the dinosaur preserve."

Dowling and Portia looked at each other.

The boy went on. "He winked and said he couldn't tell a boy, but he could tell a man." He squeezed shut his eyes. Mucus clogged his warbly voice. "I took the things he offered. I played with playing cards. I drank intoxicating liquor. I fornicated with harlots."

"And then he told you...?"

"He wanted to hunt dinosaurs. Before, he'd done it the right way, paying a fee for a permit. But if the dinos went walkabout off the preserve, he could bag them for free. And if I helped them go walkabout, he'd pay me a dinkum wage. I told myself every Sunday I'd tithe every quid he paid me. Almighty God, I was a fool. You can launder money but you can't launder sin."

"He put you in a tough spot," Portia said. A shard of anger spiked up her spine, carrying the winner cow's mounted head like an *hors d'oeuvre* on a skewer. She exhaled and kept her voice sympathetic. "How did you help them go walkabout?"

"There were four of us." He named the other three.

"They live around here?" Dowling asked. "About your age?"

"Between here and Blenheim. I was the youngest," the boy said, then shook his head as if that were no excuse. "He'd have us turn off our neurys and communicate with each other and him encrypted through short-range radio. We'd open the perimeter gate and enter the preserve on foot. We'd track them. Wasn't hard. They're active all winter and they don't expect hunters those weeks. A lot of the females are sitting their nests."

The boy swallowed. "We'd herd them through the perimeter gate to the back paddock. The four-legged ones with armored plates, minmis and kunbarrasaurs, were easy. Stupid and timid. The flightless bird-like ones too. We lured the stralla with a side of a riddlepig dead of natural causes. Towed the dead pig behind a one-man four-wheeler."

His voice cracked like a thin eggshell. "Only the winner was a challenge. Put me in awe that Almighty God once made something so bonzer. She moved quickly for something so huge. One of me mates almost got his foot stomped."

Portia spoke. "What about the cameras and microphones at the preserve's perimeter?"

"I asked Martinson about it. He laughed it off. Said he had a bloke inside company security in Blenheim who'd scrub the data."

She shivered inside her jacket. "What was the bloke's name?"

"Martinson didn't say."

Did he need to? Someone like the special agent could interrogate everyone working in security in Blenheim and unearth the turncoat.

And speaking of *unearth*... a chill flowed through her gut, but she didn't shiver. Instead she felt numb. "What happened at the back paddock?"

"We shut the gate and herded them toward the woods on the back slope." For three slow breaths he looked that direction in the darkness. "Martinson waited in a blind. We cleared out from downrange and he fired. Easy peasy," he added. Shame flooded his voice.

"Did he have you do more?"

"We'd skin them, butcher them, and measure them for taxidermy right where he felled them. The skins went off to the barn. He flew a bloke in all the way from Cookland."

Dowling rubbed against the grain of his beard stubble. "Martinson didn't say this bloke's name, either."

"That'd be right. I remember some of how he looked. A couple centimeters shorter than you. Nose long and narrow and tipped up at the end like a waterslide. He had all the equipment in the barn to make the mannequins and mount the skins. The meat, we'd carve off hunks and cook them over a firepit. The winner's ribeye, medium rare, it melted in my mouth...."

His lips and jaw worked. Portia guessed the boy's mouth watered. Then his torso convulsed in waves. He leaned away from them and retched. Foul sounds, a bilious stench. Her nose wrinkled and she had to look away.

"There's another question I have to ask," said the special agent. "What did you do with the rest of the dino carcasses?"

The boy spoke in a monotone, as if only fumes remained in his emotional fuel tank. "We had earth-moving equipment. Just like Dad talked about on the veranda with you. The bedroom window was cracked wide enough I could hear every word."

"We gathered that," Dowling said.

A breeze skittered through the oak branches above. Portia shivered again. She hadn't even thought about how the boy had learned they investigated Martinson.

"The earth movers scraped out pits," the teenager said, "shoved the carcasses in, then scraped the dirt back over. I didn't control the machinery. I helped tamp down the dirt and lay sod on top. And rig up grow lights to make sure the sod would take by summer."

Dowling turned to Portia. A quick dip of her chin confirmed what she'd guessed. The boy's testimony, along with their other evidence, would give them a warrant to search Martinson's farm. To uncover the skeletons and rotting flesh of dinos killed for a rich young man's vanity. Even if the dead dinos were only a wedge to punish Martinson for a more heinous crime, he would be punished, and their bones could lie more restfully under the impartial scales of justice.

The boy shifted against the tree trunk. He regarded Portia and Dowling. The wan light from the flashlight lit up a flicker of hope, but then his pimpled face slumped and his shoulders fell. "What comes next?"

"Your mum and the good Lord might forgive you," Dickinson said, "but you still violated Dinosaur Hunting Act 2749. I've got to tell your parents and then take you in for that."

The boy bowed his head. "I sinned. I have to pay the price for it."

Overhead, the rustle of branches eased. The air lay still in the grove. Yet still Portia shivered, more violently than before, like a dishrag getting poison wrung out. "An-an-and you threatened a fronto with a deadly weapon!"

Dowling laid his palm on Portia's forearm. He gave the boy a firm but clement look. "The ref can keep the whistle in his pocket and call advantage on that one, I think."

Portia dropped from her knee. Her rump landed on the cold ground. She hugged herself and leaned toward Dowling. Thank God the special agent knew what to do.

"Can you walk, mate?" he asked the boy.

A nod. The boy staggered to his feet. He steadied himself with one hand on the oak's ribbed trunk.

Dowling picked up the rifle and slung it over his shoulder. "Go first."

Another nod. The boy trudged, gaze cast down on the ground, through the grove of oaks. They soon came to open paddock. A thousand meters away, the few lights of the Yeardleys' farmhouse faintly glowed, outshone by the glittering sprawl of the south polar stars. In the distance, kilometers behind Portia, sounded the protective bellow of a winner bull.

ABOUT THE AUTHOR

I'M **RAYMUND EICH.** I use my Middle American upbringing as a launchpad for journeys to the ends of the Universe.

Growing up in the Midwest prepared me for my academic career, culminating with a Ph.D. in biochemistry from Rice University. It helps me help inventors prosper from their progress in medicine, biotechnology, and computer hardware.

Above all, it inspires me to write science fiction and fantasy about ordinary people facing extraordinary wonders and horrors, battling enemies both foreign and domestic, and building better lives for themselves, their families, and their societies.

My last name has one syllable and is pronounced "eye-sh." I live in Houston with my family.

Connect with me at **www.raymundeich.com** or follow the QR code below.

Online and brick-and-mortar bookstores around the world list millions of books, with thousands more published every day. I'm glad you discovered this one.

If you'd like to know when I release a new book, instead of leaving it to chance, join my Readers Club. I'll email you every two months with publishing news, an off-beat patent, and a short personal update. Plus, I'll let you know about an older book of mine you might have missed.

Yes, please! I'll go to **www.raymundeich.com/mailing-list** or scan the QR code below.

No thanks. I'll take my chances next time I look for your books.

OTHER BOOKS BY THE AUTHOR

Available wherever books are sold.

Learn more about these titles at our website, **www.cv2books.com,** or follow the QR code below.

Portia Oakeshott, Dinosaur Veterinarian

As a girl, Portia Oakeshott dreamed of caring for the reconstructed dinosaurs roaming the preserve near the south pole of her hot home planet, New New South Wales.

As a graduate from the planet's top veterinary school and a recent hire by the dinosaur company, caring for dinosaurs brings Portia into conflict with ranchers, spoiled children, villainous millionaires, religious fanatics, and politicians. Her adventures take her from the "big smoke" to the "back of Bourke"—from the bustling city of Port Bounty, across a continent of vast fields where farmers raise pigs containing cloned human organs, to the lush Cretaceous forests at the bottom of a world.

Riddlepigs and the Cryla

As a new hire at the dino company, Portia's first call sends her to an isolated farmhouse and across the perimeter into the preserve itself, in pursuit of a rogue carnivore, a female *Cryolophosaurus*. A cryla.

Amid a forest of ferns and cycads, Portia learns a lesson never taught by her professors at veterinary school. A lesson in what "caring for dinosaurs" really means.

Coming Soon
Minnie and the Trekker

Kunbarra and the Whiteants

Loovy and the Lava

Novels

The Progress of Mankind

Stone Chalmers, Book 1

Complete four-book series available

Stone Chalmers. Spy. Assassin. Instrument maintaining Earth's dominion over all human worlds.

Opposing him? Hostile forces on colony worlds... and within the Earth government itself.

Take the Shilling

The Confederated Worlds • Book 1

Complete trilogy available

Tomas seeks an escape from his backwater planet and his widowed mother's rigid religious home.

'Taking the shilling' - enlisting as a space soldier - is only the start.

The Blank Slate

Neuroscience entrepreneur Clay Shieffer must stop a tyrannical president…
because he unwittingly gave the tyrant power over the human mind.

New California

After New California's founder committed suicide, two men vied to rule the
colony.

Ashwin George, supported by the colony's elite and the Chinese company
dominating half the settled galaxy.

Against him, Desmond Park, nanotechnology engineer, armed with the most
formidable weapon of all.

A single idea.

The Reincarnation Run

Skeptical spacejock Landry Krieger knows exactly how to smuggle the
"reborn" spiritual leader of an oppressed people past their conquerors... but the
boy's priests—and governess—shake up his orderly plans.

Azureseas: Cantrell's War

Ross Cantrell joined the animal control mission on the newly-discovered planet
Azureseas to earn the money to start married life together with his girlfriend.

Then Ross discovers the truth about the planet's "animals."

Short Novels

The ALECS Quartet

He had a month to learn the planet's mysteries—and Juliette's.

His cover story: return to Elard to dismantle his sect's missionary work to the planet's natives.

His true mission: investigate decades-old mysteries of love and death.

His objective: return to Earth with his discovery.

If he can.

A Mighty Fortress

Theodore and his team from the Lutheran Interstellar Terraforming Society would transform a barren, rocky world into a refuge of faith and life.

Or die trying.